nickelodeon

 A GOLDEN BOOK • NEW YORK

The stories contained in this work were originally published separately by Golden Books as follows: *Mr. FancyPants!,* in 2009, adapted by Geof Smith and illustrated by Caleb Meurer, based on the screenplay "To SquarePants or Not To," by Luke Brookshier, Nate Cash, and Steven Banks; *Dora's Birthday Surprise!,* in 2010, written by Molly Reisner and illustrated by Dave Aikins; and *Roller Rintoo!,* in 2010, adapted by Geof Smith and illustrated by Jason Fruchter, based on the screenplay "Roller Rintoo," by Chris Nee.
SpongeBob created by

Stephen Hillenburg

www.randomhouse.com/kids

Educators and librarians, for a variety of teaching tools, visit us at
www.randomhouse.com/teachers

ISBN: 978-0-375-87227-3

MANUFACTURED IN SINGAPORE

10 9 8 7 6 5 4 3 2

Mr. FancyPants!

SpongeBob opened his front door and greeted another beautiful Bikini Bottom morning.

"It's a perfect day," he said. "A perfect day for chores!"

SpongeBob loved to . . .

dust,

wash,

and vacuum.

"It's laundry day, Gary!" SpongeBob said.
He collected all his square pants—and even Gary's
pants, too—and filled the washing machine.

While the clothes were drying, Patrick called.
"Hi, SpongeBob," he said. "Listen to how long
I can whistle."

SpongeBob learned that Patrick could
whistle for a long, **long**, **long** time.

Gary got his pants out of the dryer in time, but SpongeBob waited too long. All his pants had shrunk!

"Gary, it looks like I need to get new pants," SpongeBob said.
Gary said, *"Meow."*

Unfortunately, the pants store at the mall was all out of SpongeBob's style! And there wasn't going to be another shipment of square pants for *months*!

Then SpongeBob found a pair of pants he liked. In fact, he thought they were perfect. "They hug me like my mother!"

On the way back home, SpongeBob
ran into Patrick. "Notice anything different?"
SpongeBob asked.

"Who are you?"

"I'm SpongeBob!"

Patrick thought for a moment.

"SpongeBob has **square** pants. Now leave
me alone, you mysterious stranger."

"Patrick's so full of tartar sauce," SpongeBob said to himself. "I'm still SpongeBob! It's just a different pair of pants."

But then Sandy didn't seem to recognize him, either.

"You sure look like **Mr. FancyPants**!" she said with a laugh.

SpongeBob wasn't too worried, because he knew that Patrick and Sandy could be pretty silly sometimes. But when Squidward didn't recognize him, he got scared.

(Actually, Squidward did recognize SpongeBob. He was just trying to ignore him.)

"These pants are more powerful than I expected!" SpongeBob cried. "I guess I'm not SpongeBob SquarePants anymore. I'll have to start all over! I'm ready! I'm ready! I'M READY!"

The first thing SpongeBob FancyPants
needed was a job. So he went to the place he
knew best: the Krusty Krab.

The moment SpongeBob FancyPants walked
in, Mr. Krabs told him to get to work.

"I've got the job!" SpongeBob shouted.

"SpongeBob FancyPants has never worked here before," he said. "So you have to tell me what to do. Teach me everything you know!"

"Hmmm," Squidward whispered to himself. "Maybe I can get him fired. Then he'll leave me alone."

So SpongeBob FancyPants learned to do everything around the Krusty Krab— just the way Squidward did it.

SpongeBob ignored the customers.

And he made fun of the food.

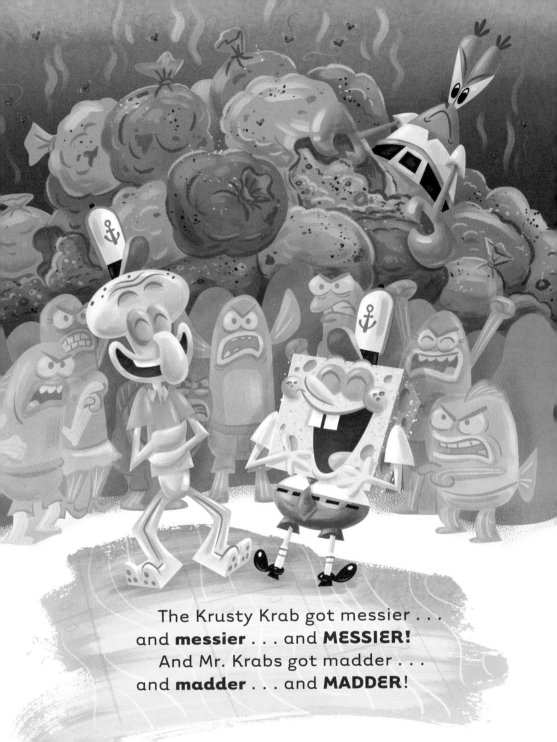

The Krusty Krab got messier . . .
and **messier** . . . and **MESSIER!**
And Mr. Krabs got madder . . .
and **madder** . . . and **MADDER!**

"I'm used to Squidward doing a terrible job!"
Mr. Krabs yelled. "But I expect more from *you*,
Mr. SquarePants!"

"But I can't be SpongeBob SquarePants with
ROUND PANTS on!" SpongeBob cried.

"Well, take them off," Mr. Krabs said.

"Whatever you say, Mr. Krabs!"

"I guess I'm SpongeBob **UnderPants** from now on!"

Dora's Birthday Surprise!

¡*Hola!* I'm Dora, and this is my best friend, Boots. Today is a day that only comes once a year—my birthday!

Look! Silly Mail Bird has a message for me. Let's read it together.

Dear Dora,
¡Feliz cumpleaños! Happy birthday!
Get ready for your Birthday Scavenger Hunt! We have a present for you, but you'll have to look for three clues to find it. We'll all celebrate together when you find the last clue.
Love,
Mami and Papi

A scavenger hunt! *¡Fantástico!* Will you help me look for clues? Great!

I wonder where we should start looking. Who do we ask for help when we don't know which way to go? *¡Sí!* Map!

Map says that the first clue is in the tallest tree in the Nutty Forest. The second clue is at Troll Bridge. And the third clue is on top of Rainbow Rock. *¡Vámonos!* Let's go!

Hey! There's Tico! Tico says he'll give us a ride to the Nutty Forest. *¡Gracias, amigo!* Thanks!

We made it to the Nutty Forest! Now, which tree is the tallest?

Yeah, the tree in the middle is the tallest!
¡Excelente!

Boots climbed up
the tallest tree to look
for the first clue. Great
climbing, Boots!

There's a box hanging from a branch. Help Boots climb to the branch. *¡Sube, sube!* Climb, climb!

There's a ball of yarn inside the box! The yarn is my first clue. Let's look for the next one.

We need to go to Troll Bridge for the second clue. But first we have to get through the Purple Gate. Will you check Backpack for something that will open the lock? Say "Backpack!"

"Do you see anything that will open the lock?

Yeah, that's right, the purple key! *¡Muy bien!*"

We're at Troll Bridge! The Grumpy Old Troll says we have to solve his riddle to get the box. Will you help?

*"This dessert is sweet
And a birthday treat to eat.
But first it needs to bake.
It's a birthday . . ."*

Hmm. What's a sweet dessert you
bake and eat on a birthday? *¡Sí!* A CAKE!

Uh-oh! Swiper wants to swipe the box that's holding my second birthday clue!

He says he won't swipe my box because it's my birthday. *¡Gracias, Swiper!*

Now let's see what's inside the box. It's a little bowl! The first clue was a ball of yarn, and the second clue is a bowl. I wonder what my present is. Let's go find the last clue at Rainbow Rock!

¡Mira! Look! There are stars everywhere!
Artista, the Skywriting Explorer Star, wrote
a birthday message for me in the sky!

BIRTHDAY!

How many stars do you see? *Uno, dos, tres, cuatro, cinco, seis, siete, ocho, nueve, diez.* Ten stars! We need to reach up and catch the stars. Reach high in the air! Super catching!

We're at Rainbow Rock! To get to the top, we need to climb the colored rocks. Do you see them?

Call out the color of each rock to show us which way to go! Red! Orange! Yellow! Green! Blue! Purple! *¡Fantástico!*

We made it to the top! Do you see a box
hidden anywhere? There's a box in that bush.
Let's open it to find the last clue!

The third clue is a carton of milk! What are all the clues, again? Yarn, a bowl, and milk. What do you think Mami and Papi got me? I have an idea. . . . I really hope I'm right! Let's find out at my party!

Yay! All my friends and family are at my birthday party. Mmm, Papi made a chocolate cake! I'm making a wish before I blow out my candles. What will you wish for on your birthday?

¡Mira! I was right! Mami and Papi gave me a kitten—just like I thought the clues were telling me! I'm going to name him Gatito. He loves playing with the yarn and drinking milk from his bowl!

Thanks for helping me find the birthday clues and for coming to my party! *¡Gracias!*

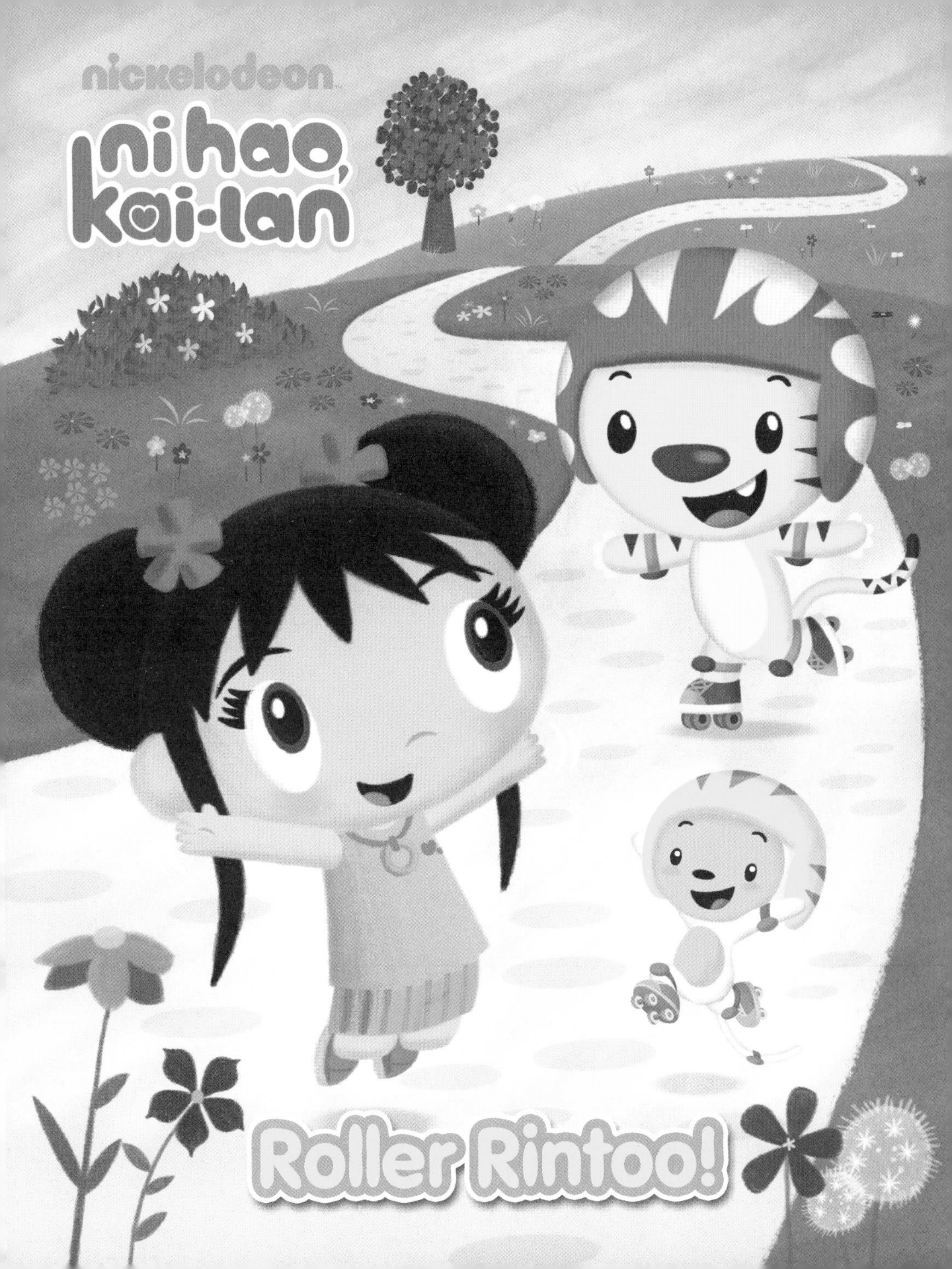
nickelodeon
ni hao, kai-lan
Roller Rintoo!

Ni hao! I'm Kai-lan!

Do you know what I'm doing today? I'm putting on a helmet and pads and my skates so I can go skating at the roller rink! Do you like to skate?

YeYe is my grandfather. He's a great roller skater. He always helps me put on my skates and pads. *Xie xie,* YeYe.

Sometimes skating can be a little tricky.

It's a good thing YeYe is here to help.
He reminds me to start slowly.

Now I've got it! I can skate really *fast!*

Do you know how I
say *fast* in Chinese? *Kuai.*

Here come Tolee and Hoho—and they're ready to skate! I really like their helmets.

We can skate uphill,

downhill,

and all around the park.

Look! There's Rintoo!

Rintoo wants to go to the roller rink, too.
He hasn't skated before,

but he's a fast runner

and a great
jumper.

He thinks skating will be easy.

Let's go, go, go to the roller rink!

Look! Lulu is on her skateboard. She's just
learning, so she's going slowly and letting
Mr. Fluffy and Mei Mei help her. Good luck, Lulu!

Rintoo can't wait to put on his skates.

Do you think he's excited to start skating?

Rintoo is ready to go.

Watch out!

It looks like skating is harder than Rintoo expected.

We want to help Rintoo, but he says he can skate by himself.

Oh, no! Rintoo threw off his skates.

Do you think he's unhappy because skating is so hard?

We were right. Rintoo wants to be a great skater, but it is really hard. What can we do to help?

I have an idea! Let's ask Lulu. She just started skateboarding by herself, and she's already really good. Let's find out how she did it.

Lulu started by going really slowly.

Then Mei Mei and Mr. Fluffy helped her. First with two hands . . .

then with one hand . . .

then with no hands!
Now she's a super skateboarder!

Rintoo is going to try to skate again. He's starting slowly, and Tolee and I will help.

First we'll use two hands . . .

then we'll use one hand.

Wow! Rintoo doesn't need any more help. He can skate by himself!

He's ready to skate at the roller rink! Great job, Rintoo! *Zhen bang!*

Wow! Rintoo's a super skater. Everyone's having a great time. The lightning bugs are here to put on a roller-rink light show!

Thank you for helping us show Rintoo how to skate. You make my heart feel super happy. Goodbye! *Zai jian!*